What's Michael?

Off The Deep End

Written and Illustrated:
Makoto Kobayashi

English translation:
Dana Lewis, Jeanne Sather,
and **Toren Smith**

Lettering and art retouching:
L. Lois Buhalis

English version produced by **Studio Proteus** for **Dark Horse Comics, Inc.**

Editor:
David Land

Designer:
Mark Cox

publisher
Mike Richardson
executive vice president
Neil Hankerson
vice president of publishing
David Scroggy
vice president of finance
Andy Karabatsos
general counsel
Mark Anderson
creative director
Randy Stradley
director of production & design
Cindy Marks
art director
Mark Cox
computer graphics director
Sean Tierney
director of sales & marketing
Michael Martens
director of licensing
Tod Borleske
director of m.i.s
Dale LaFountain
director of human resources
Kim Haines

Published by
Dark Horse Comics, Inc.
10956 SE Main Street
Milwaukie, OR 97222

First edition: October 1997
ISBN: 1-56971-248-4

10 9 8 7 6 5 4 3 2 1
Printed in Canada

MICHAEL'S DISASTER

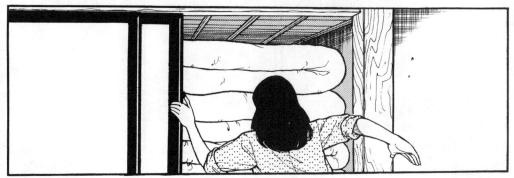

DANCING MICHAEL!!

PART ONE

THE FIRST TIME I SAW IT... ...MICHAEL WAS CHASING A FLY.

"WHEN THE FLY CAME OUT FROM UNDER THE TABLE, IT FLEW UP...

AND THEN *IT* HAPPENED!"

BZZZZZ

KONK

. . . .

THAT'S THE WHOLE STORY, SWEAR TO GOD!

THAT'S UNBELIEVABLE! HAS IT EVER HAPPENED AGAIN?

"SURE HAS! JUST THREE DAYS AGO, I HEARD A CRASH IN THE LIVING ROOM...

SKRASSH

Hm...?

"I WENT TO CHECK ON WHAT IT WAS..."

Hn...?

. . . . !

"AND WHEN I LOOKED INTO THE LIVING ROOM, I DISCOVERED HE'D KNOCKED OVER A FLOWER VASE!"

BUT...BUT THIS IS JUST *INCREDIBLE!!* WHAT AN AMAZING CAT!

Aw, NO... HE'S JUST AN OLD ALLEY CAT WE FOUND! HA HA HA!

WOW! WE'D GIVE *ANYTHING* TO GET A PICTURE OF HIM DANCING!

WELL, NOW... THE QUESTION IS, WILL HE DO IT? I'VE ONLY SEEN HIM DANCING TWICE, AND I'M AROUND HIM EVERY DAY...

PLEASE! SOME-HOW! *ANYTHING!!*

YOU KNOCKED HIM OUT, YOU, YOU *BEAST!*

YOU DIDN'T HAVE TO HIT HIM SO *HARD!*

GEEZ, DO YOU HAVE ANY BETTER IDEAS?

THE *LAST* TIME HE BUMPED HIS HEAD, HE DANCED, DAMMIT!

....!

MICHAEL!

MICHAEL, DEAR!!

N*YO*WLL....!

MORAL: THOU SHALT NOT FORCE CATS TO DO TRICKS...

END.

DANCING MICHAEL!!

PART TWO

WELCOME TO THE CATHOUSE

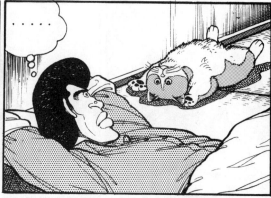

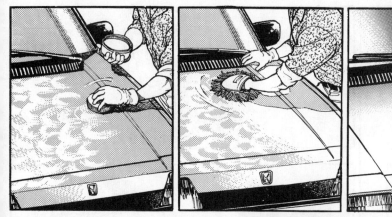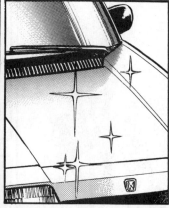

THE NEW CAR

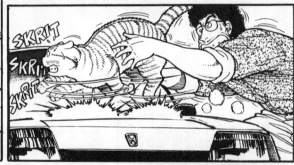

KRAK

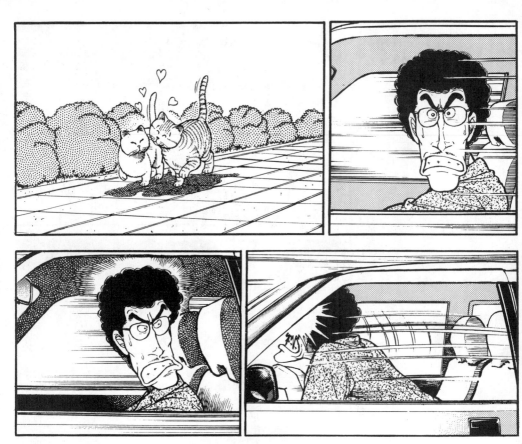

The MEETING

CONFOUND IT! DON'T GROOM YOUR TAIL DURING A MEETING!

MICHAEL! YOU'RE OUR BUSINESS MANAGER! EXPLAIN THIS FIASCO!

.....

.....

MROW?

DON'T YOU "MROW" ME!

OUR COMPANY IS ON THE ROPES!

.....

YOU! STOP THAT YAWNING!!

THE SALES OF OUR RIVAL, K-9 CORP, ARE GOING THROUGH THE ROOF!

THEY'RE EVEN BUILDING A NEW HEADQUARTERS!

BAM

KWIK

SPLSSH

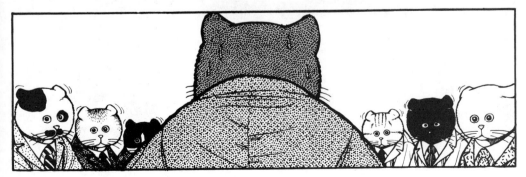

HAIL AND FAREWELL

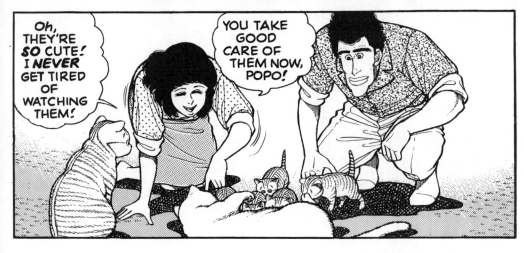

Hmm?

BINGG
BONGG

JUST
A
MO-
MENT!

KREEE

I...
I...
WE...

C-C-CAN
I
H-HELP
YOU?!

NOW, THEN, MA'AM, DON'T YOU WORRY A BIT.

WE'LL TAKE CARE OF 'EM GOOD, AND SEND YOU PICTURES EVERY MONTH!

TH-THANK YOU, SIR...

meww ...?

meww ...?

PLEASE ...

BE NICE TO THEM!

. . . .

IT-- IT REALLY IS BETTER THIS WAY, I KNOW...

THAT'S RIGHT, HONEY! YOU'VE GOT TO BELIEVE... THEY'LL BE MUCH HAPPIER THIS WAY!

YEAH...

MICHAEL! POPO!

I KNOW YOU MUST BE MISSING THEM BADLY, BUT--

A MOVEABLE FEAST

MICHAEL LENDS A PAW

BEST OF FRIENDS, REVISITED

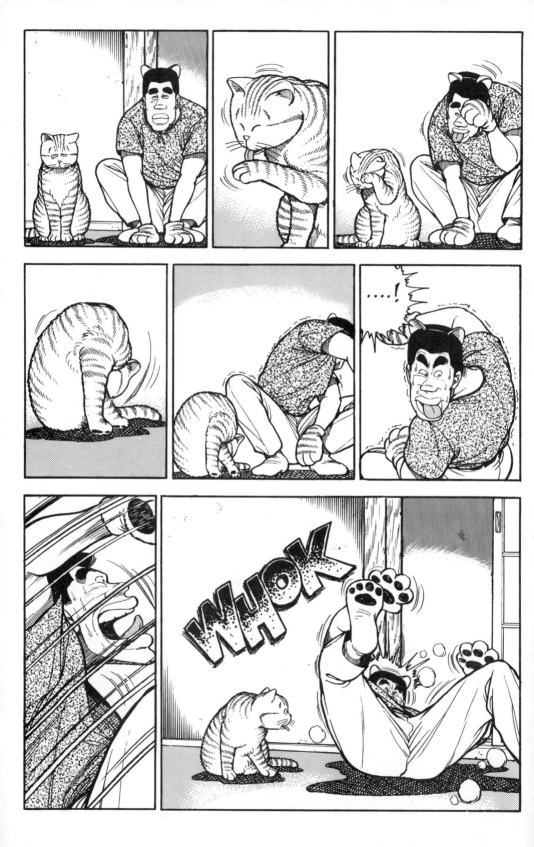

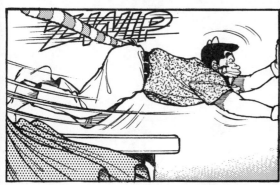

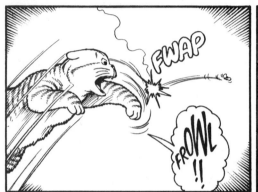

FATHER KNOWS BEST

As you can see...

...Michael was a father again.

HE WANTED TO PLAY, TOO, BUT HIS DIGNITY AS A FATHER REQUIRED HIM TO REFRAIN.

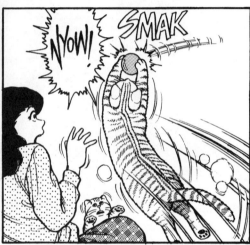

IT WAS HIS SPECIAL PLACE... BUT AS A FATHER, HE HAD TO THINK ABOUT HIS CHILDREN FIRST.

AW, YOU DON'T HAVE TO HIDE IN THE CORNER!

COME ON, MICHAEL.

. . . . .

IT'S TOUGH BEING A DAD...

A CAT OWNER HAS TO KNOW HER PET...

THE YAKUZA*, PART THREE:

THE MELANCHOLIA OF MR. "M"

* The Japanese Mafia

A MEMBER OF THE YAKUZA. JUST CALL HIM "M"...

HIGH HONCHO IN THE KODANSHA GANG...

HE'S NOT AFRAID OF ANYTHING...

≒ulp≒
...

?!

...!

...!

...!

≒hahh≒
≒hahh≒

JUST A DAMN CAT, BUT I'M SO SCARED, I'VE GOT A NOSEBLEED!

WHAT--

--WHAT IF THE NEW RECRUITS SAW ME LIKE THIS...?

AND...

AND EVEN WORSE...

WHAT IF I TURN THAT CORNER...

AND THERE'S A CAT CURLED UP ON A CUSHION IN THE MIDDLE OF THE STREET?! WHAT SHOULD I DO???

A-AND...

WHAT IF THAT CAT TURNS HIS HEAD...

AND HE HAS SLIT PUPILS?!

TH-THEN WHAT SHOULD I DO??

OR... EVEN WORSE...

≈hahh≈
≈hahh≈

WHAT IF MARI GOES AND BUYS A CAT...

A-AND I SPEND THE NIGHT THERE AND SHE SERVES TOAST IN THE MORNING...

AND SOME BUTTER DRIPS ON MY FOOT...

PLIP!

N'YOW...?

AND THE CAT LICKS IT OFF... !?!

SLUP

WHAT SHOULD I DO??!

MY... MY GOD...   A-AND...

WHAT IF I BREAK INTO K'S PLACE...

K!! TIME TO DIE!!!

BAM

!!

FWAP

...AND K IS SLEEPING WITH A C-CAT?!? WHAT'LL I DO??

AND... IF...

≥hahh≤
≥nahh≤

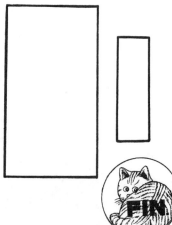

A "MICHAEL" PRIMER

Summer

Winter